Dear Mrs. LaRue

Letters from Obedience School

Written and Illustrated by

Mark Teague

Scholastic Inc. New York

The Snort City

September 30

For Tracy Mack, Brilliant Editor;
David Saylor, Impeccable Designer; and Earl and Ali, Dogs of Genius

This book was originally published in hardcover by Scholastic Press in 2002.

ISBN 978-1-338-78196-0

12 11 10 9 8 7 6 5 4 3 2 1   22 23 24 25 26 27

Printed in the U.S.A.   76

This edition first printing, March 2022

The display type was set in American Typewriter Bold. The text type was set in 14-point ITC American Typewriter Medium and 18-point Litterbox. The illustrations were painted in acrylics.

Register/Gazette

LOCAL DOG ENTERS OBEDIENCE SCHOOL

"Ike"
LaRue

Citing a long list of behavioral problems, Snort City resident Gertrude R. LaRue yesterday enrolled her dog, Ike, in the Igor Brotweiler Canine Academy. Established in 1953, the Academy has a history of dealing with such issues.

"I'm at my wit's end!" said Mrs. LaRue. "I love Ike, but I'm afraid he's quite spoiled. He steals food right off the kitchen counter, chases the neighbor's cats, howls whenever I'm away, and last week while I was crossing the street he pulled me down and tore my best camel's hair coat! I just don't know what else to do!"

School officials were unavailable for comment. . . .

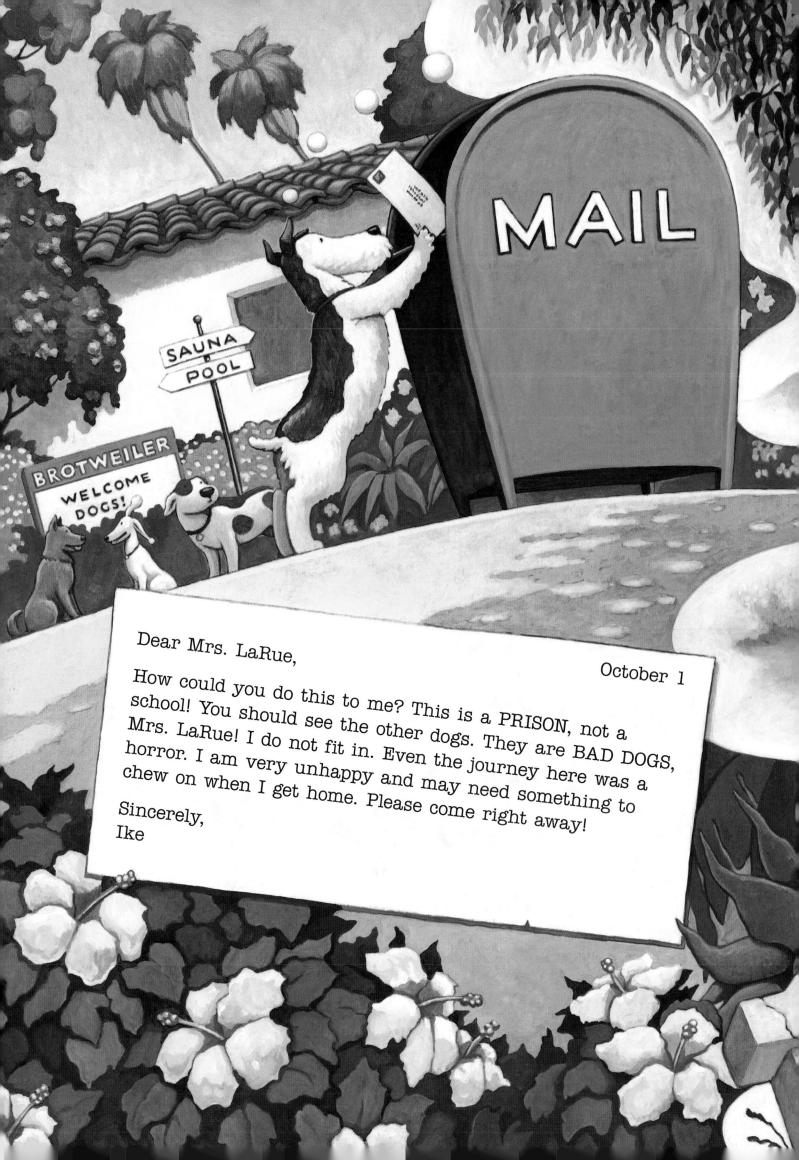

Dear Mrs. LaRue,   October 1

How could you do this to me? This is a PRISON, not a
school! You should see the other dogs. They are BAD DOGS,
Mrs. LaRue! I do not fit in. Even the journey here was a
horror. I am very unhappy and may need something to
chew on when I get home. Please come right away!

Sincerely,
Ike

Dear Mrs. LaRue,

Were you really so upset about the chicken pie? You know, you might have discussed it with me. You could have said, "Ike, don't eat the chicken pie. I'm saving it for dinner." Would that have been so difficult? It would have prevented a lot of hard feelings. Needless to say, I am being horribly mistreated. You say I should be patient and accept that I'll be here through the term. Are you aware that the term lasts TWO MONTHS? Do you know how long that is in dog years?

Sincerely,
Ike

Dear Mrs. LaRue,

I'd like to clear up some misconceptions about the Hibbins' cats. First, they are hardly the little angels Mrs. Hibbins makes them out to be. Second, how should I know what they were doing out on the fire escape in the middle of January? They were being a bit melodramatic, don't you think, the way they cried and refused to come down? It's hard to believe they were really sick for three whole days, but you know cats.

Your dog,
Ike

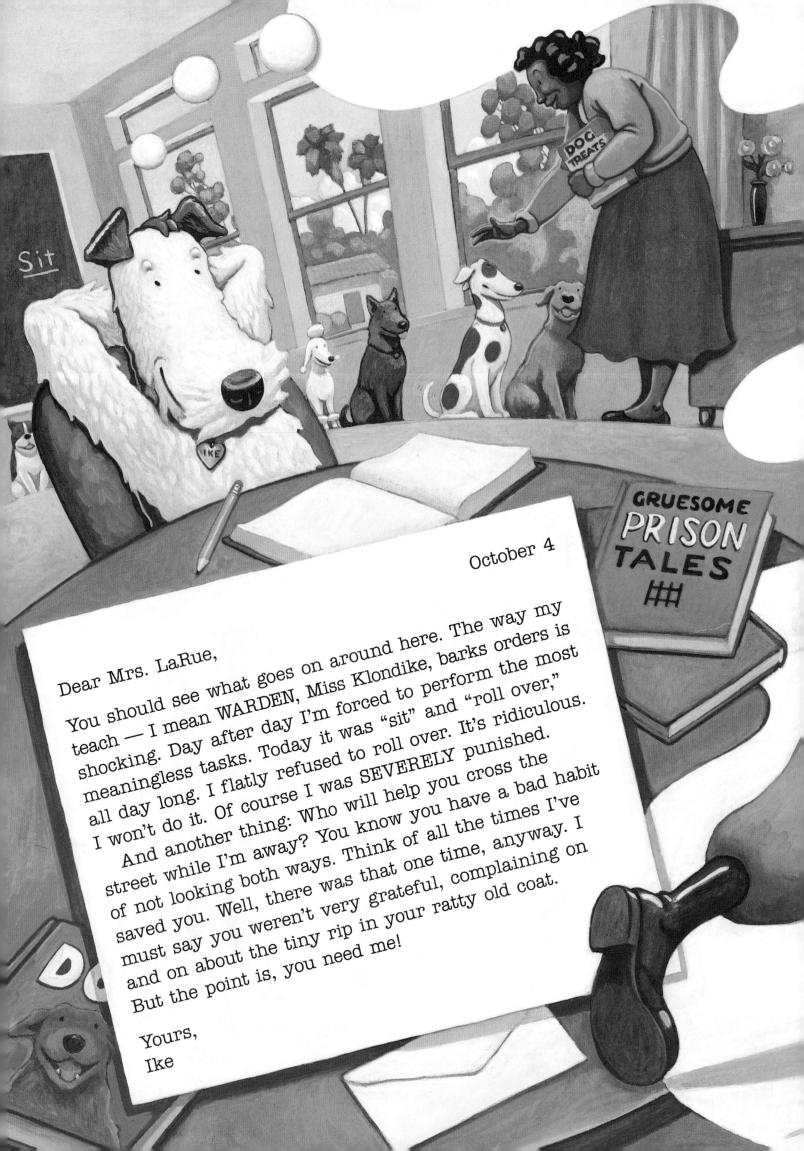

Sit

October 4

Dear Mrs. LaRue,

You should see what goes on around here. The way my teach — I mean WARDEN, Miss Klondike, barks orders is shocking. Day after day I'm forced to perform the most meaningless tasks. Today it was "sit" and "roll over," all day long. I flatly refused to roll over. It's ridiculous. I won't do it. Of course I was SEVERELY punished.

And another thing: Who will help you cross the street while I'm away? You know you have a bad habit of not looking both ways. Well, there was that one time, anyway. I saved you. Think of all the times I've must say you weren't very grateful, complaining on and on about the tiny rip in your ratty old coat. But the point is, you need me!

Yours,
Ike

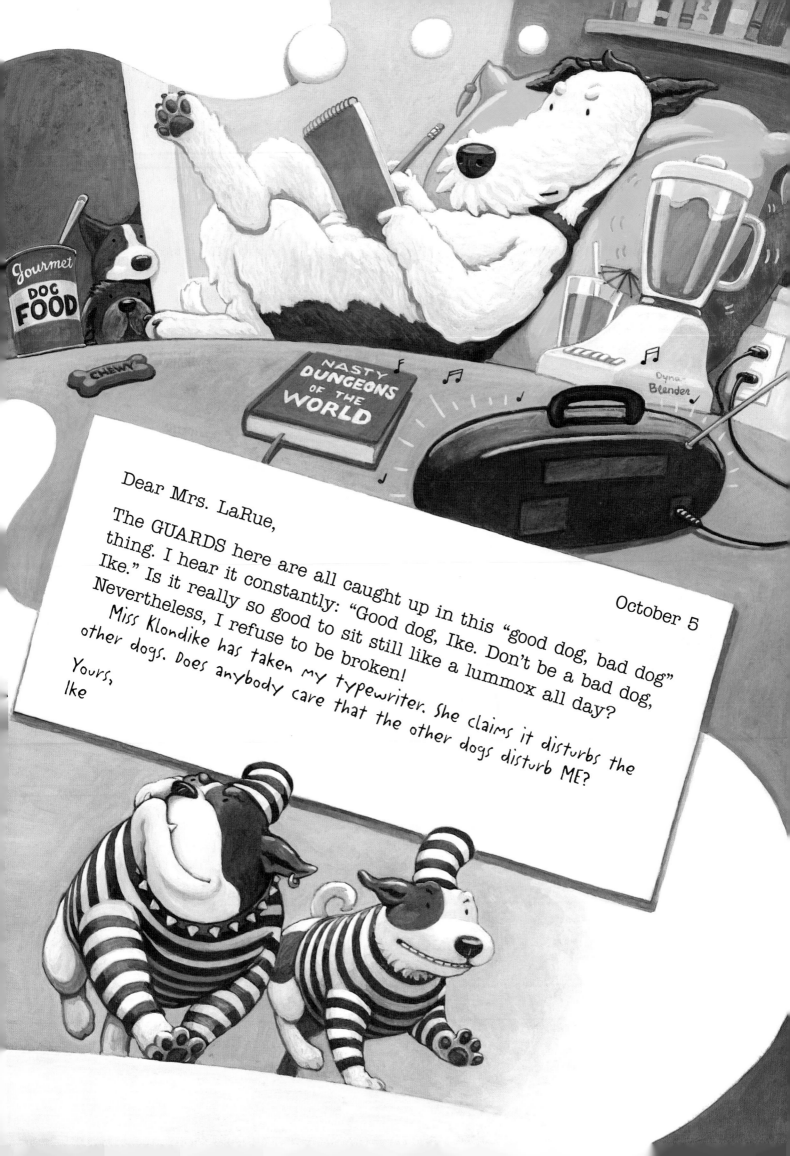

Dear Mrs. LaRue,   October 5

The GUARDS here are all caught up in this "good dog, bad dog" thing. I hear it constantly: "Good dog, Ike. Don't be a bad dog, Ike." Is it really so good to sit still like a lummox all day? Nevertheless, I refuse to be broken!

Miss Klondike has taken my typewriter. She claims it disturbs the other dogs. Does anybody care that the other dogs disturb ME?

Yours,
Ike

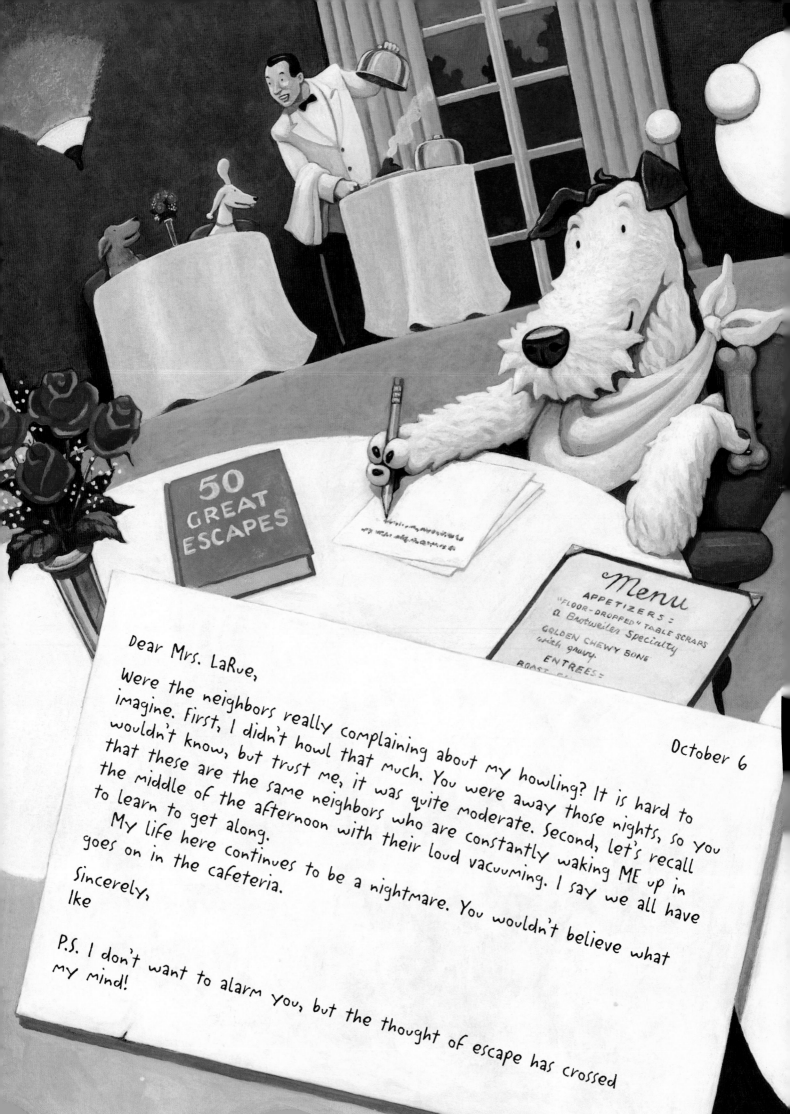

50 GREAT ESCAPES

Menu
APPETIZERS:
"FLOOR-DROPPED" TABLE SCRAPS
a Rottweiler Specialty
GOLDEN CHEWY BONE
with gravy
ENTREES:
ROAST

Dear Mrs. LaRue,

October 6

Were the neighbors really complaining about my howling? It is hard to imagine. First, I didn't howl that much. You were away those nights, so you wouldn't know, but trust me, it was quite moderate. Second, let's recall that these are the same neighbors who are constantly waking ME up in the middle of the afternoon with their loud vacuuming. I say we all have to learn to get along.

My life here continues to be a nightmare. You wouldn't believe what goes on in the cafeteria.

Sincerely,
Ike

P.S. I don't want to alarm you, but the thought of escape has crossed my mind!

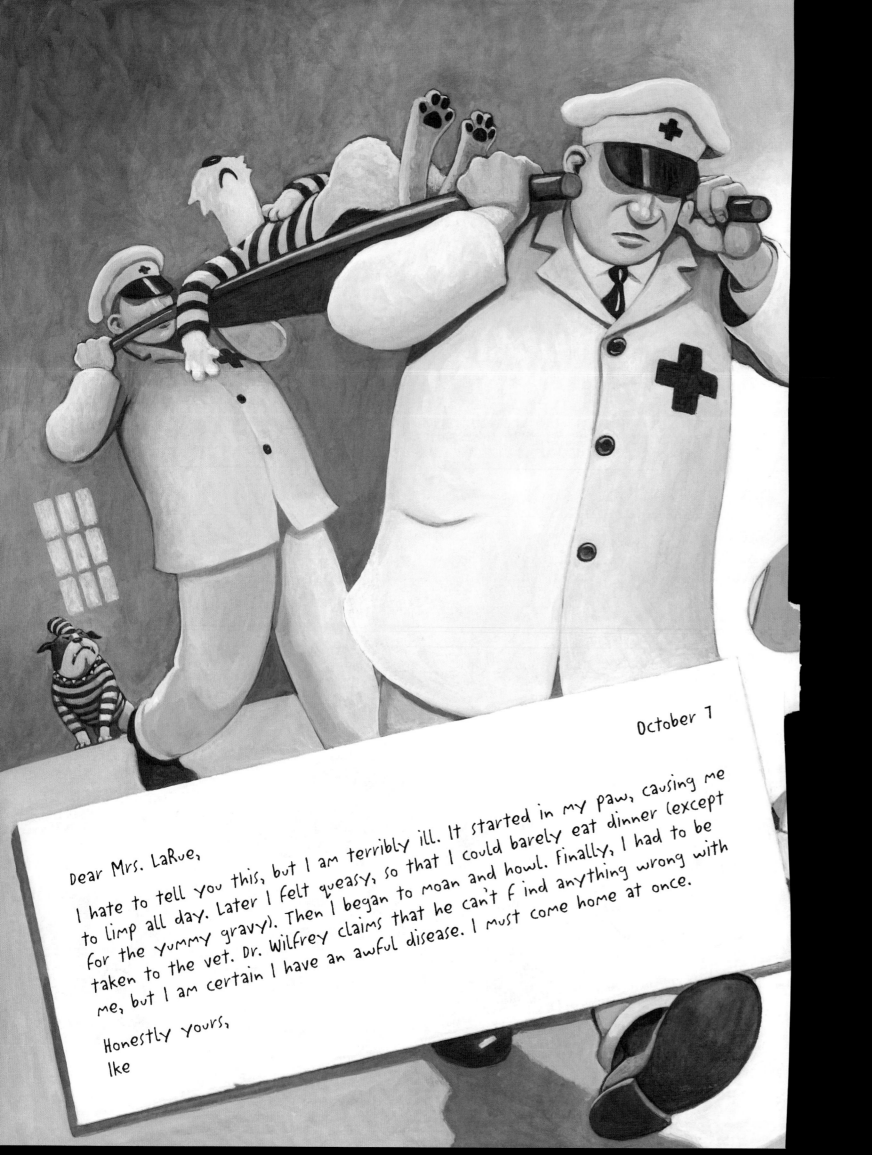

October 7

Dear Mrs. LaRue,

I hate to tell you this, but I am terribly ill. It started in my paw, causing me to limp all day. Later I felt queasy, so that I could barely eat dinner (except for the yummy gravy). Then I began to moan and howl. Finally, I had to be taken to the vet. Dr. Wilfrey claims that he can't find anything wrong with me, but I am certain I have an awful disease. I must come home at once.

Honestly Yours,
Ike

October 8

Dear Mrs. LaRue,

Thank you for the lovely get well card. Still, I'm a little surprised that you didn't come get me. I know what Dr. Wilfrey says, but is it really wise to take risks with one's health? I could have a relapse, you know.

With fall here, I think about all the fine times we used to have in the park. Remember how sometimes you would bring along a tennis ball? You would throw it and I would retrieve it EVERY TIME, except for once when it landed in something nasty and I brought you back a stick instead. Ah, how I miss those days.

Yours truly,
Ike

P.S. Imagine how awful it is for me to be stuck inside my tiny cell!
P.P.S. I still feel pretty sick.

October 9

Dear Mrs. LaRue,

By the time you read this I will be gone. I have decided to attempt a daring escape! I'm sorry it has come to this, since I am really a very good dog, but frankly you left me no choice. How sad it is not to be appreciated! From now on I'll wander from town to town without a home — or even any dog food, most likely. Such is the life of a desperate outlaw. I will try to write to you from time to time as I carry on with my life of hardship and danger.

Your lonely fugitive,
Ike

The Snort City Register/Gazette

LARUE ESCAPES DOGGY DETENTION

Former Snort City resident Ike LaRue escaped last night from the dormitory at the Igor Brotweiler Canine Academy. The dog is described as "toothy" by local police. His current whereabouts are unknown.

"To be honest, I thought he was bluffing when he told me he was planning to escape," said a visibly upset Gertrude R. LaRue, the dog's owner. "Ike tends to be a bit melo-dramatic, you know. Now I can only pray that he'll come back." Asked if she would return Ike to Brotweiler Academy, Mrs. LaRue said that she would have to wait and see. "He's a good dog basically, but he can be difficult. . . ."

October 11 — Somewhere in America

Dear Mrs. LaRue,

I continue to suffer horribly as I roam this barren wasteland. Who knows where my wanderings will take me now? Hopefully to someplace with yummy food! Remember the special treats you used to make for me? I miss them. I miss our nice, comfy apartment. But mostly, I miss you!

Your sad dog,
Ike

P.S. I even miss the Hibbins' cats, in a way.

October 12 — Still Somewhere

Dear Mrs. LaRue,

The world is a hard and cruel place for a "stray" dog. You would scarcely believe the misery I've endured. So I have decided to return home. You may try to lock me up again, but that is a risk I must take. And frankly, even more than myself, I worry about you. You may not know it, Mrs. LaRue, but you need a dog!

Your misunderstood friend,
Ike

The Snort City Register/Gazette

October 13

HERO DOG SAVES OWNER!

Ike LaRue, until recently a student at the Igor Brotweiler Canine Academy, returned to Snort City yesterday in dramatic fashion. In fact he arrived just in time to rescue his owner, Gertrude R. LaRue of Second Avenue, from an oncoming truck. Mrs. LaRue had made the trip downtown to purchase a new camel's hair coat. Apparently she neglected to look both ways before stepping out into traffic.

The daring rescue was witnessed by several onlookers, including patrolman Newton Smitzer. "He rolled right across two lanes of traffic to get at her," said Smitzer. "It was really something. I haven't seen rolling like that since I left the police academy."

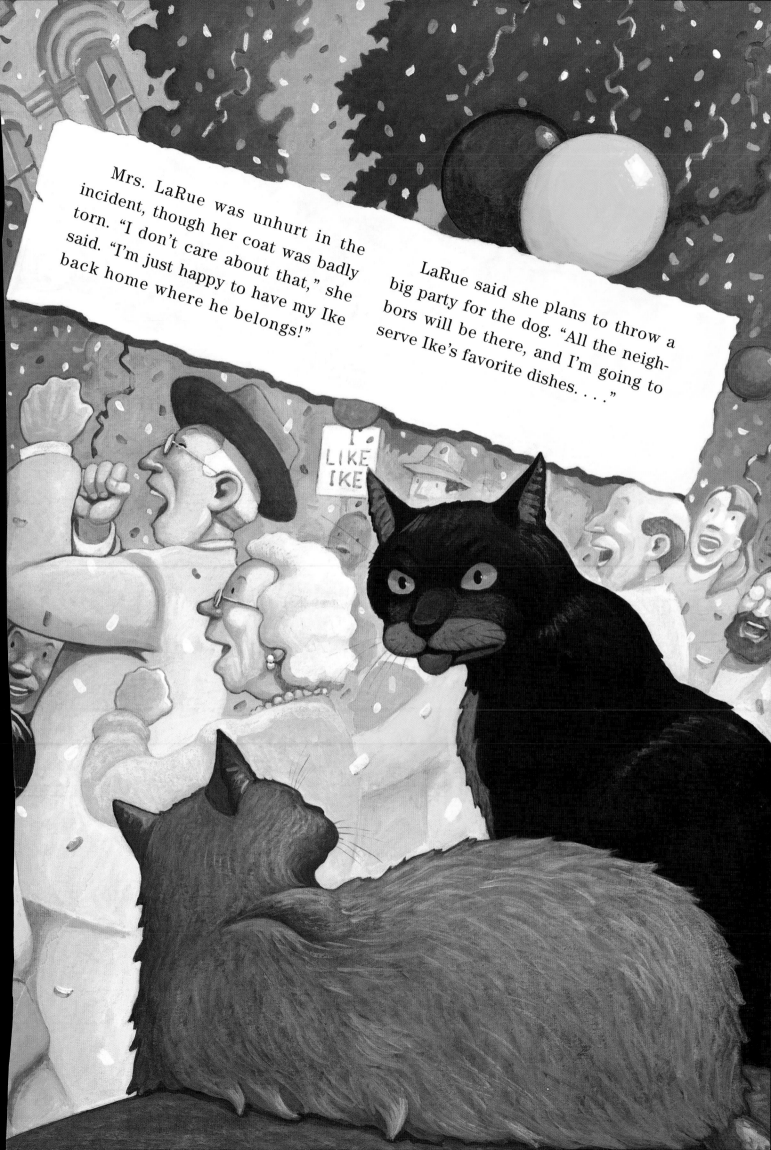

Mrs. LaRue was unhurt in the incident, though her coat was badly torn. "I don't care about that," she said. "I'm just happy to have my Ike back home where he belongs!"

LaRue said she plans to throw a big party for the dog. "All the neighbors will be there, and I'm going to serve Ike's favorite dishes. . . ."